My seventh Enid Blyton book

By the same author

My first Enid Blyton book
My second Enid Blyton book
My third Enid Blyton book
My fourth Enid Blyton book
My fifth Enid Blyton book
My sixth Enid Blyton book
My eighth Enid Blyton book

Also available for younger readers

The Boy Who Turned into an Engine
The Book of Naughty Children
A Second Book of Naughty Children
Ten-Minute Tales
Fifteen-Minute Tales
Twenty-Minute Tales
More Twenty-Minute Tales
The Land of Far-Beyond
Billy-Bob Tales
Tales of Betsy May
Eight O'Clock Tales
The Yellow Story Book
The Red Story Book
The Blue Story Book
The Green Story Book
Tricky the Goblin
The Adventures of Binkle and Flip
Mr Pink-Whistle's Party
Merry Mr Meddle
Mr Meddle's Mischief
Don't Be Silly Mr Twiddle
Adventures of the Wishing Chair
More Adventures of the Wishing Chair
Rag Tag and Bobtail
Tales from the Bible
Children's Life of Christ
Bedtime Stories and Prayers

Enid Blyton

My seventh Enid Blyton book

DRAGON
Granada Publishing

Dragon Books
Granada Publishing Ltd
8 Grafton Street, London W1X 3LA

Published by Dragon Books 1984

First published by Macmillan and Co Ltd, London, 1942

ISBN 0-583-30711-6

Printed and bound in Great Britain by
Collins, Glasgow

Set in Times

Contents

The stories in this book and in My eighth Enid Blyton book *were first published in* I'll tell you a story *by Macmillan and Co Ltd in 1942.*

The old shipwreck tree

IN Bluebell Wood there stood an old oak tree that was very easy to climb. Mollie and John called it the Shipwreck Tree, because they used to pretend that when they were up in its branches they were on a raft out at sea, looking for land.

'We've been shipwrecked, Mollie,' John said. 'Our ship has gone down, and we are on a raft, looking out for an island where we can land safely and find coco-nuts to eat.'

'And perhaps treasure hidden on the island!' said Mollie. 'Ooh, what fun!'

They used to climb up very high and then look out over the countryside, pretending that it was all sea. Then suddenly Mollie would shout:

'Land ahoy! Land ahoy!'

It was a most exciting game, and whenever they could go to Bluebell Wood they always ran to the old Shipwreck Tree and climbed it. The wind swayed them about in the tree, and they felt just as if they were on the sea, being swayed about by the waves.

One afternoon they went to Bluebell Wood together. They ran to the Shipwreck Tree and climbed it to play their favourite game.

'I'll be Captain this time, Mollie,' said John. 'It's my turn. Now let's talk about our poor ship that went down.'

'Oh dear, oh dear,' said Mollie, 'what a dreadful shipwreck that was! How fortunate that we were able to get off on a raft before the ship sank!'

'But we may die of hunger and thirst before we reach land!' said John, pretending to be very worried. 'Did we bring any food, Mollie?'

'Not a crumb!' said Mollie, sighing deeply. 'Oh, if only we could see land somewhere! Look again, John!'

John stood up on his branch and looked over the countryside.

Suddenly he shouted in excitement:

'Land ahoy! Land ahoy!'

'Hurrah!' cried Mollie. 'We will land

and find some coconuts to eat, and perhaps some bananas.'

'And maybe we'll find some treasure to take back home when we're rescued!' said John.

'Ooh, I wish we could,' said Mollie. 'It's nice to pretend, John, but I do wish we could *really* find some treasure, don't you?'

'It only happens in books,' said John. 'Come on, let's go down and pretend to explore the island. Bump! We've landed on the shore, Mollie. Get off the raft.'

Mollie was just going to scramble down when John caught hold of her arm. 'Sh!' he said in a whisper. 'There's somebody coming. Let's pretend there are savages on the island! We'd better stay here till they've gone!'

As quiet as mice the two children sat up in the tree. They heard the sound of someone moving in the wood below. Then a man carrying a sack came into sight. And goodness me, he sat down right under the Shipwreck Tree! How the

children hoped he wouldn't look up and see them!

Then they heard more footsteps and soon another man came up to the first one. They began to talk in very low tones. The children could hardly hear a word, but they felt sure that the men were wondering what to do with their sack.

'Well, it's best to hide it here for the night,' said the first man at last, in a louder voice. 'No one will come to this spot till to-morrow, anyhow.'

'All right. Put it under that thick gorse bush there,' said the second man. They moved off to a thick bush and pushed the sack underneath it. They pulled the bush down over it to hide it, and then they went off together.

The children looked at one another. What an adventure! What was in that sack? They were very glad the men hadn't seen them!

'Is it safe to land and find the treasure, Captain?' whispered Mollie.

'I'll just look and see if the savages have gone!' said John. He stood up in the tree. 'Yes! They are going down the lane beyond the wood. It's all clear!'

Down scrambled the two excited children, and ran to the gorse bush. They pulled out the sack and opened it. And whatever do you think there was in it! Silver spoons and forks, silver dishes and vases, and silver cigarette boxes!

'Goodness! Those men must have been burglars!' said John. 'We'd better tell the police. Come on. We can't carry the sack

– it's too heavy. Help me to take it to another bush; then if the men come back they won't find it where they hid it!'

They hid it under another bush and then ran off to the village. They went to the policeman's house and told him what they had found. He went back with them to Shipwreck Tree and pulled out the sack.

'Yes!' he said. 'It's a whole lot of things that have been stolen from people's houses lately! Aha! I'll fill the sack with stones and get another man here to watch for those thieves to come back. What a surprise they'll get!'

He popped the things into another sack he had brought and went home with the children. He told their mother what they had done, and she was very proud of them

'I expect Uncle Dick's silver cigarette box is among those things,' she said. 'He had it stolen last week. How pleased he will be to get it back!'

The two thieves were caught when they went back for their sack. All the things were taken back to their owners, and everyone was told about the two children up in the Shipwreck Tree.

And one day what do you think arrived in the postman's van? You'll never guess! Why, a real raft, a proper one that would float! With it was a note signed by all the people who had got back their stolen things, and this is what the note said: 'With love to Mollie and John, hoping they will find it useful next time they are shipwrecked!'

How excited those two children were! They took the raft straight out to the big duck pond, and floated it. It held them both quite safely, and away they sailed on the pond, scattering all the ducks.

I hope they won't *really* be shipwrecked, don't you?

Skippo's prank

SKIPPO was an elf who lived in a tiny shop not far from the royal palace. He sold dancing-spells at sixpence a time. They were very good little spells for those who wanted to dance and didn't know how to.

'All you have to do,' Skippo would say, 'is to put one of my little spells in your shoe. Then you will find that your legs will do most beautiful dances, and you will not feel ashamed because you don't know how to dance.'

Skippo sold a lot of spells, and with the money he bought his food and clothes. He was very fond of fried onions and he cooked these every night for himself.

Now when he left his kitchen door and window open the wind often blew the smell of his frying onions into the window of Princess Goldilocks's nursery, at the back of the Fairy King's palace. She didn't like the smell at all, and her maid begged the King to ask Skippo to close his door and window when he wanted to cook his onions.

So the King sent for Lord High-and-Mighty, the Chamberlain, and told him go at once to Skippo's shop and tell him about the onions.

Lord High-and-Mighty was annoyed at having to go. He thought that one of the footmen could have gone. But as he didn't dare to disobey the King, he set off, frowning hard, and stepping out slowly and haughtily.

He was a big Chamberlain, stout and red-faced, and his clothes always looked as if the buttons were bursting off. He walked down the village street in his high boots, looking down his nose at everyone, until he came to Skippo's shop.

He went inside and rapped loudly on the counter. Skippo ran to see what was wanted.

'Skippo,' said Lord High-and-Mighty, 'please shut your door and window when cooking your disgusting onions each evening. The smell makes the Princess feel faint, and the King is very angry about it.'

Now this was untrue, for although the Princess didn't like the smell, it certainly didn't make her feel faint, and the King wasn't at all angry.

Skippo went red.

'My onions aren't disgusting,' he said. 'They're as good as yours!'

'I don't eat onions,' said the Chamberlain. 'Nasty, common things! Ugh! Only horrid little elves like you eat such things!'

'Tell that to the King!' said Skippo

rudely. 'Why, he had onions with his steak the other day. I know, because the cook told me, and she's my sister. So there, Mr Clever!'

Well, you should have seen the Lord High Chamberlain's face. It really was quite green! 'I shall go at once to report your rudeness to His Majesty!' he said, and he turned to go.

Skippo was frightened. He knew that he had no right to speak like that. Quick as lightning he ran to the door and

opened it. He bowed low as the Chamberlain stalked out, and he slipped a little dancing-spell into one of the Chamberlain's high boots as he passed by! Lord High-and-Mighty didn't see him – oh no, he was too quick for that.

Half-way down the street the spell began to work. You should have seen the Chamberlain! His legs suddenly began to throw themselves about! They kicked and stamped, they jigged and jumped, taking him along with them. He was too surprised to say a single word!

How everyone stared! Then they all began to laugh, for the Chamberlain was nobody's favourite. They followed him down the street, and whenever one of his legs kicked very high in the air they clapped their hands in glee.

Suddenly there came a grand carriage rolling down the street. It was the King's! He was in it and so was the Queen. When they saw Lord High-and-Mighty gambolling and capering in such a strange way they exclaimed in surprise.

The King stopped the carriage and leaned out.

'What are you doing, Lord High-and-Mighty?' he asked.

'N-n-nothing! It's my legs!' said the poor Chamberlain, and to his great horror his right leg jerked itself up and kicked the King's crown off! Oh dear me, how everyone trembled to see such a thing! The King couldn't believe his eyes

'Pick up my crown at once, and stop behaving in such a silly way,' he commanded the Chamberlain. But the poor man couldn't pick up the crown, for as soon as he danced near enough to it his foot kicked the crown even further away.

'He's got one of Skippo's dancing-spells in his boot!' suddenly cried a nearby pixie. 'That's what's the matter with him. He came out of Skippo's shop. I saw him. Skippo has slipped a spell into his boot!'

The King drove at once to Skippo's shop, and very soon the naughty little elf had confessed.

'How dare you do such a thing!' roared the King. 'How dare you, I say! Pack up your spells and leave my kingdom at once. I won't have you here!'

The elf packed up his belongings and then, with the tears running down his face, he swung his sack on to his back and walked down the road to the gates of Fairyland. The Lord High Chamberlain saw him go, and he shook his fist at him, for the dancing-spell was still as strong as ever, and his legs were kicking about all over the place, making him very much out of breath.

'You can stay out of Fairyland until Lord High-and-Mighty forgives you,' said the King to Skippo. The elf sighed and wept faster than ever, for he knew that the Chamberlain would never, never forgive him.

He is in our world now with his dancing-spells. They are not strong enough for *our* legs, so who do you think he gives them to? To the little lambs in the spring time! Have you seen how they jump and frisk about, enjoying themselves enormously? It's no wonder they do, for Skippo has slipped a dancing-spell

into their little hoofs, and they skip in the sunshine as happy as can be.

Look over the hedge and watch them. If you look hard enough, you might even see Skippo, leaning against an old sheep, half asleep in the sunshine!

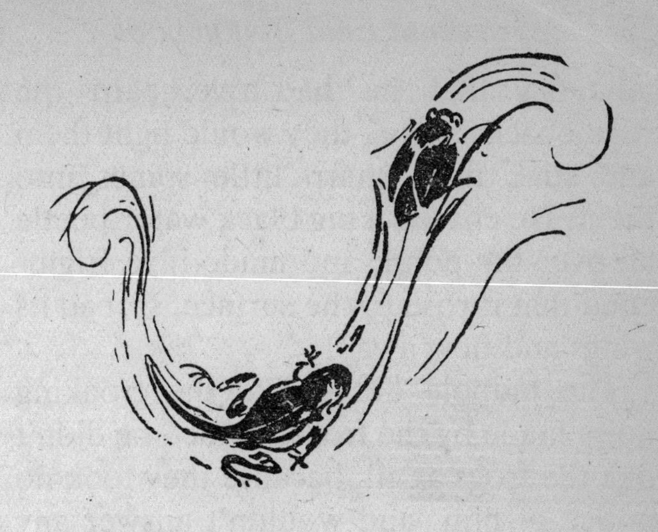

The tadpole and the duckling

THERE was once a foolish tadpole who lived in a little pond with a great many frogs, some minnows, hundreds of water-snails, six white ducks and three yellow ducklings.

He was a little nuisance, that tadpole. He would keep putting his blunt little nose into everything. He asked the snails why they wore shells, and he told the minnows that he had overheard the sticklebacks saying they would fight them and stick their sharp little spines into them. He chased a big black water-beetle all over the pond, and made it so frightened that it rose to the surface, spread its wings and flew away!

The tadpole didn't like the croaking noise made by the frogs. In fact, he didn't like the frogs at all, because they took no notice of him, and wouldn't answer any of his questions.

'Those frogs are stuck up,' said the cheeky tadpole to a water-snail. 'I'm tired of them. They take up a lot of room, they make an ugly croaking noise, and they don't take the slightest notice when I speak to them.'

'I don't wonder,' said the snail. 'I think you're a silly busybody. Go and swim with the other tadpoles and leave the frogs alone. You ought to know better than to interfere with them.'

The tadpole butted the snail with his head. He was angry – but the snail simply coiled himself up in his shell and laughed at him.

The tadpole swam off. As he went he saw a strange and frightening sight. One of the big white ducks suddenly put its head under the water, caught hold of a frog and ate him! Oh my! The tadpole shook from nose to tail.

Then he swam off to a minnow and told him what he had seen.

'Didn't you know that ducks ate frogs?' said the minnow. 'You *are* a little silly!'

'Well,' thought the tadpole, swimming off, 'I'm glad that ducks eat frogs. Yes, I am! I shall go and make friends with one of those little yellow ducklings, and then I will tell her where she can find frogs to eat. I will soon have the pond cleared of those stuck-up frogs! Ho ho!'

Silly little tadpole! He thought himself so clever and yet he didn't even know that tadpoles grew into frogs! Off he swam to the smallest yellow duckling, quite determined to do away with every single frog in the pond.

'If all those silly frogs were gone, the pond-snails and the fishes might make me their king,' thought the tadpole. 'I am clever and I know a lot. When I am a very big tadpole I shall be grand and wise. I would like to be king of the pond.'

He swam up to the duckling. She was very small, but even so she was much larger than the tadpole. She listened to all he had to say.

'I don't eat frogs yet,' said the duckling. 'I am too small. I only eater water-insects, you know. But later on, in a few weeks' time, when I am big, I shall be glad of a good meal of frogs. Be friends with me, dear tadpole, and when I am big I will be only too glad to do as you say, and eat all the frogs in the pond. Come and talk to me each morning.'

So the tadpole proudly swam to the duckling each day and talked to her. He felt so grand about it that he would hardly say a word to the minnows or the snails – and they were very glad to be rid of him. How they smiled to see him friends with a duckling!

The weeks went by. The duckling grew

big. Her feathers turned from yellow to cream. She was a pretty little duck. The tadpole altered, too. He became bigger. He grew back legs and then he grew front legs. His tail became shorter and shorter. And at last he was a little frog!

But he didn't know it. He was so proud of being friends with a duckling that he no longer talked to his brothers and sisters, the other tadpoles. They would have told him that he was already a little frog. But no, he was too grand altogether!

One day the duckling was very hungry, and she told the tadpole so.

'Ho!' said the tadpole, pleased. 'Well, would you like a good meal of frogs today? I know where some are hiding in the weed. I will take you there and you shall feast on them. The sooner they are gone the better, for I want to be king of this pond.'

'Take me to the frogs,' said the duckling eagerly. So the tadpole took her to the weed.

'Put your head under the water and

look in the weed,' he cried. 'You will see the frogs there, and can feast on them!'

The duckling did as she was told. But as soon as the frogs in the weed saw her yellow feet paddling near them they fled away fast. Only the tadpole was left, and he, of course, was no longer really a tadpole, but a little frog.

The duckling saw him and caught him in her beak, thinking him to be one of the frogs she had come to catch.

'Let me go, let me go!' cried the little tadpole-frog. 'It's me, your friend!'

'What, you're the tadpole who spoke to me!' quacked the duck. 'I don't believe it! You're a frog like the rest of them. Look at yourself.'

The tadpole saw his feet, and found that his long tail had gone. He was indeed a frog. What a dreadful thing! Who could have told him he would turn into a frog? After all his wonderful plans, it was really dreadful! How everyone in the pond must have laughed at him!

'Yes, I am a frog now,' he said sadly. 'I thought I should be a tadpole all my life. I didn't know I had turned into a frog. I was too clever. Let me go, dear duckling!'

'Not I!' said the duckling. 'You said I could eat all the frogs in the pond and I shall begin with *you*! Nobody will miss such a little silly as you, I'm sure!'

With that she tossed up her head and swallowed the foolish frog. That was the end of him.

All the fishes and the frogs who had

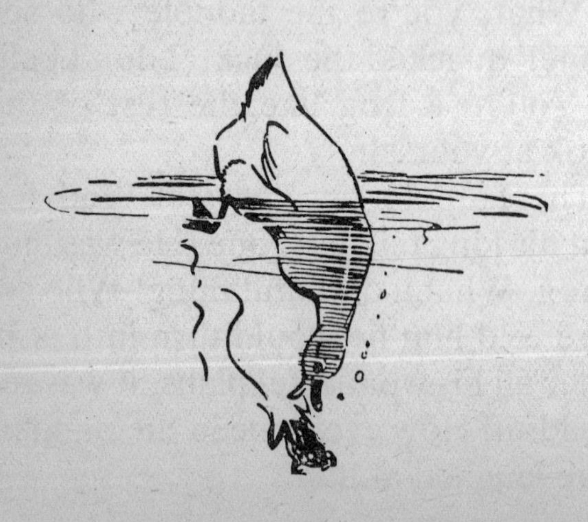

seen this shook their heads and looked solemn.

'He deserved it,' they said. 'We are not in the least sorry for him.' And neither am I!

The meddlesome toys

PETER came into the nursery with his kite and flung it down on the floor.

'I can't fly this kite properly,' he said to his mummy. 'It isn't made quite right. Perhaps Daddy can alter it for me so that it will fly nicely.'

'Well, put it away in the cupboard and I'll ask him,' said Mummy. 'I think there is something wrong with it myself. Daddy can easily put it right for you.'

Peter threw the kite into the toy cupboard. It was very cross. When night came it began to grumble.

'There's nothing wrong with me!' it said. 'I'm all right. That boy can't fly me properly, that's all!'

Now there really *was* something wrong with the kite. It would fly up a little way and then would dive down with a bump. It hadn't been made properly. But the kite went on grumbling.

'I'm quite all right. It's that silly boy. If any of you toys knew how to fly me, I'd soon show you I was all right,' said the kite.

Now the teddy bear had rather a good opinion of himself. 'Well,' he said, 'I'm sure *I* could fly you. I've sometimes thought that Peter is really rather stupid. Fancy not being able to fly a kite! We toys could, I'm sure!'

'Don't be so conceited,' said a lazy little voice – it was the toy cat who was speaking. 'Peter's as clever as any other boy of seven! You're not nearly as clever as he is, Teddy, so be quiet.'

'Ho!' said the bear angrily. 'So I'm

conceited, am I? I couldn't fly the kite, you say? Don't be silly!'

'Yes, don't be silly,' said the curly-haired doll, who was very fond of the teddy. 'You talk too much, Cat.'

'If the bear says he's clever enough to fly the kite, I believe him,' said the fluffy elephant, waving his trunk about.

'So do I,' said the big wooden soldier.

'Well, I think the *cat* is right,' said the timid bunny. 'Anyway, what does it matter? None of us is going to be so silly as to try to fly the kite, surely!'

'Ho, is that what you think?' asked the bear rudely. 'Well, think again, Bunny. It's a fine windy night and I'm going to take the kite and fly him, so there!'

'And we'll come with you!' cried the curly-haired doll, the fluffy elephant and the wooden soldier.

'You're welcome to go!' said the cat, the bunny, the clown and the Dutch doll. 'You'll be sorry, that's all, for trying to be so clever!'

The bear said nothing more. He picked

up the excited kite and marched out of the nursery followed by the elephant, the soldier and the doll. He went into the garden, and made his way to a little hillock, still followed by his friends.

'Where's the string?' said the bear. 'Oh, here it is. Now we'd better all hold on to it, because if the kite flies high, as it surely will, I shan't be strong enough to hold it myself.'

'Are you ready, Kite?' called the elephant.

'Yes,' said the kite. 'I'm waiting for the next puff of wind. Unwind a good bit of string, please.'

The wind came. Puff! The kite flew up into the air, and the wind gave another puff. Higher still flew the kite, and the

teddy bear tried to unroll the string – but, alas, he got it into a knot, and couldn't undo it. Puff! went the wind again, and the kite flew higher still.

The teddy bear was dragged off his feet, and the elephant, the doll and the soldier were jerked into the air, too, holding on to the string for all they were worth! What a shock for them!

Puff! The wind blew again, and the

kite dragged all the toys through the air.

Then it suddenly lost its balance and dived down to the ground, just as it had kept doing with Peter that morning. Bump! It struck its head on the ground and lay still.

The toys fell to the earth, too – but alas for them, the duck-pond was just below them, and they all fell into it – splash!

It wasn't very deep, and they waded out, very muddy and very wet. They didn't say a word to each other. They picked up the kite and walked home.

There was still a little fire in the nursery, and the toys sat down close to it, shivering.

'Whatever have you been doing?' asked the toy cat in astonishment.

'Nothing,' said the bear crossly.

'They couldn't fly me after all,' said the kite angrily. 'Silly creatures! They hung on to the string, and pulled me down!'

'We *didn't* pull you down!' cried the doll. 'You dragged us over the pond and then made us fall into it. You're a mean nasty kite!'

'Ha ha!' laughed the cat and the bunny.

'Ho ho!' roared the clown and the Dutch doll. 'What a joke! So you all fell into the duck-pond! Well, it serves you right for meddling!'

The other toys said nothing. They were still cold and wet. They dried themselves as best they could, and then crept back to the toy cupboard, quite ashamed of themselves. They knew perfectly well they shouldn't have meddled with the kite.

In the morning Peter and his Daddy came into the nursery and Peter pulled out his kite.

'See, Daddy,' he said, 'there's something wrong with it.'

'Yes,' said his Daddy. 'This string should be tied *here*, look – and this one *here*! Then the kite will be all right. It could never fly as it was. Nobody could fly it, not even me!'

'Did you hear that?' whispered the toy cat to the bear, giving him a nudge. 'Well, Mr Clever, no wonder you couldn't fly the kite last night! Ho, Mr Meddlesome, what a silly you are!'

The teddy bear said nothing but he went red right to the back of his ears.

'Squeak!' said the bunny in his timid little voice. 'Mr Bear, you're not so clever as you thought you were! Ho ho!'

The bear rubbed a tear out of his blue glass eyes. He didn't like being laughted at.

'GRR-rrr-rrr!' he said. 'I shan't meddle again, I promise you!'

And he didn't!

The money-box pig

THE pig that stood on the nursery mantelpiece wasn't just a pig – he was a money-box, too. In the middle of his back was a slit and pennies and half-pennies slipped in there quite easily. He felt a very light pig when he was empty, and a very heavy pig when he was full.

The toys didn't think much of him, and hardly ever spoke to him, which hurt him very much. And then when the toys planned a fine party one night and didn't ask the money-box pig to go, he was dreadfully offended.

'Why can't I come?' he shouted from the mantelpiece. 'I want to come!'

'Only toys are coming,' said the golly. 'You're not a toy.'

'Well, what am I, then?' asked the pig crossly. 'I'm not a real pig, am I?'

'No,' said the golly.

'And I'm not an ornament, like a vase of flowers, am I?' asked the pig.

'No,' said the golly. 'I don't know what you are, but you're not a toy, so we don't want you. You're a silly creature, with your pink spots and your curly tail.'

The pig nearly burst with rage.

'What about you, with your black face and staring eyes?' he shouted, dancing about on the mantelpiece till all the pennies inside him rattled and clinked.

'Be quiet – you'll wake the children!' said the golly angrily. 'And don't say such rude things to me. I may have a black face and staring eyes, but Philip and

Mollie are very fond of me. They both love me dearly.'

'And don't they love me, too?' asked the pig.

'How could they love a creature like you, covered with silly pink spots, and made of cold china?' asked the golly scornfully. 'Nobody could hug a thing like you!'

The money-box pig thought his heart was broken when he heard the golly say that the children didn't love him. Didn't he guard their precious pennies for them? Didn't he stand up all day on the mantelpiece holding their heavy pennies? Well, well, well, it was a sad thing to hear that they didn't love him after all he did for them.

'If they don't love me, I don't want to stay here,' he said sadly. 'I shall go away to some other nursery where the children will like a money-box pig. Goodbye, toys, I shan't see you again.'

The little money-box pig walked along the mantelpiece, climbed down the back

of a chair and jumped on to the floor. All the pennies rattled and he nearly fell over.

He walked along the floor to the door. The toys stared after him as he went out.

'You shouldn't have been so unkind to him,' said the bear to the golly. 'He isn't a bad little chap really.'

'And he's awfully good at looking after the children's pennies,' said the big doll.

'I don't know what Philip and Mollie will say when they find that their money-box is gone,' said the clockwork clown. 'He's got all their money inside him, you know. They are saving up to buy their mother a birthday present, and they will be dreadfully upset to find it's all gone with the money-box pig.'

'Ooh my!' said the golly in dismay. 'Of course he's got the money with him. Goodness, now what are we to do?'

'It was your fault for being so unkind to him,' said the white rabbit. 'You'd better go and get him back before he falls into a puddle and gets drowned.'

'Well, none of you wanted him to come to our party tonight,' said the golly, 'so it's as much your fault as mine. We'd better all go after him.'

So off they all went, out of the nursery door. They found the pig crying by himself at the top of the stairs. They were too steep for him to climb down.

'Pig, don't run away,' begged the golly. 'We want you back.'

'Think how upset Philip and Mollie will be in the morning to find you and their pennies all gone,' said the big doll.

'You s-s-said that the ch-ch-children didn't l-l-love me!' wept the little pig.

'Of course they love you and trust you, or they wouldn't give you their pennies to hold,' said the clown. 'They never give *us* their pennies – only you. You are very honoured.'

The pig cheered up a little

'Well, I'm glad you think the children do love me a little,' he said. 'But I think I'll run away, all the same, because I don't like living in a nursery where the toys think I'm not worth asking to parties. Goodbye. Tell the children I'm sorry to take their pennies with me, but I don't know how to get them out of my middle.'

He took a few steps towards the stairs. The golly pulled him back and put his arm round him.

'Dear money-box pig,' he said, 'listen to us. We are fond of you really. We don't want to lose you.'

'Will you ask me to your party then?' said the pig.

'Yes, you shall come,' said the golly.

'But I haven't anything pretty to wear,' said the pig, beginning to cry again. 'I shall feel funny without a party dress.'

'The golly shall let you wear his red coat,' said the doll. 'It was he who sent you away, so he ought to do something to make up for it. You shall wear his red coat.'

'I should like that,' said the pig. He and all the toys walked back to the nursery. The doll made the golly take off his fine red coat, and they put it on the pig. He poked his front legs through the sleeves, and looked very grand indeed.

They had a glorious party. The pig danced so much that all the pennies inside him jingled like mad. In fact, he danced so gaily that he didn't hear the cock crow! So he couldn't get back to the mantelpiece in time, and when the cock crew he fell fast asleep in the middle of the nursery floor, still wearing the golly's red coat! He did look funny.

Philip and Mollie found him there when they ran into the nursery in the morning – and how astonished they were!

'Look! Pig's got Golly's coat on!' cried Mollie. 'And how did he get from the mantelpiece to the floor? What a funny

thing! Hallo, little money-box pig! We've come to take out the pennies inside you today, because we're going to buy Mummy's birthday present this morning!'

Well, wasn't the little pig glad that he hadn't run away after all, when he heard that! He knew that the children would have been very unhappy if they hadn't been able to go and buy their present. He beamed at them and nearly danced round the nursery with joy.

'You shall keep your red coat on,' said Philip, putting him back on the mantel-piece. 'You look fine in it!'

Poor Golly! He hasn't got his coat back yet! But he shouldn't have been so mean to the little money-box pig, should he?

What happened to a smile

BENNY was a thin little boy, and he had never had an overcoat in his life. He had only once had a penny to spend, and he had never forgotten that day. He was quite happy, though, and what his mother would do without him she really didn't know.

'You know, Mother,' said Benny, 'I really don't mind being poor except for one thing – and that is I can never give anybody anything! I can't give Lucy next door a Christmas present at Christmas time, and I can't give Tom a birthday present. I can't even give the old blind man at the corner a halfpenny, and I wish I could.'

'Why, Benny!' said his mother, in surprise. 'What does it matter if you can't give people presents and money? You can give them other things, can't you?'

'What things?' asked Benny.

'Well, you can give them a bright smile, for instance,' said his mother. 'You can give them a hand with their parcels. You can say a polite "Good morning" to the people in the road. Look at that poor, ugly old Mr Grim who lives in the next street – nobody ever smiles at him, and I'm sure he must be sad and lonely, without a friend in the world!'

Benny thought about what his mother said. Yes, it was quite true. Although he hadn't any money at all to buy things for other people, he could give smiles and kindness. He made up his mind to begin that very day.

He went out shopping for his mother that morning. He took her string bag with him, because she wanted some potatoes. As he went he kept a look-out for old Mr Grim. Benny was really a bit frightened of him, because he had such thick, shaggy eyebrows, and he frowned so crossly.

Sure enough, down the street came Mr Grim, frowning hard, as usual. And just as he reached Benny the little boy raised his cap, said 'Good morning,' most politely, and smiled. Benny had a fine smile.

It made you feel happy and good when he smiled at you.

Mr Grim was so surprised that he forgot to smile back. He just stared at Benny as if he couldn't believe his eyes. The little boy went on his way, glad that he had smiled, but disappointed that Mr Grim hadn't smiled back.

'It was a waste of a smile!' said Benny to himself. But it wasn't. A smile is never wasted – never. Hear what happened to this one, and you'll see.

Mr Grim went on his way. He kept thinking of Benny's smile, and it warmed his cold, lonely heart. When he got home he went and looked at himself in the mirror. He saw a dirty, untidy, cross old man there. Dear, dear, what a dreadful sight he looked!

'There must be something nice about me, or that little boy wouldn't have given me such a fine smile,' said Mr Grim to himself. 'Well, I've always thought I was an ugly, cross, sour, bad-tempered old fellow who hated children and hadn't a

friend in the world. I wonder – could I possibly be mistaken?'

He looked at himself again, and then a thought came into his head.

'I don't believe I'm as bad as all that!' he said. 'I believe if I was clean and tidy, and had a nice new suit and my hair cut, I'd be a fine fellow. That little chap wouldn't have smiled at me if I had been as bad as everyone makes out.'

Well, you should have seen Mr Grim that day! He took off all his things and had a hot bath. Then he put on his clothes again, and shook his head. 'I can't tidy

these up,' he said. 'I will go and get a new suit.'

So off he went. He popped into the hairdresser's first of all and had his hair cut nicely. Then he went to Mr Hem, the tailor.

'I want a nice new suit,' he said. 'Something cheerful and bright. And I want a new hat. Oh, and a new overcoat, too. Please fit me for all these things.'

Mr Hem was delighted. Things had been going very badly with him lately, and he hadn't enough work to do. He began to measure Mr Grim and he talked to him happily. So few people ever talked to Mr Grim that he felt more pleased than ever. How fine it was to get a new suit and be measured by a nice friendly tailor like this!

'I think I'll have *two* suits!' he said suddenly. 'Yes, I could really do with two. I'll have one in blue and one in a nice warm brown. And I'll have two hats as well.'

Well, Mr Hem couldn't believe his ears! What a lot of money he would make that week! Oh my, it was good news! He would be able to send his little nephew a fine birthday present now. That was good.

Mr Grim left the shop at last, beaming all over his face. Mr Hem, the tailor, sat down and set to work to cut the cloth to make the new suits.

He smiled to himself. 'What shall I send Jack for his birthday? Shall I send him a train? No, he's got one. Shall I send him a book? No, I might send him one he's got already. Dear me – what shall I send him, now?'

He cut out the sleeves of a coat and thought hard. 'I know!' he said at last. 'I will send him some money. Yes, I will send him five shillings. Or shall it be seven shillings and sixpence? He is a good boy, and I am fond of him. I shall make lots of money from these coats. I will send him seven shillings and sixpence!'

Well, when he had done a good deal more work he stopped for his dinner. Then he went out to the post office and he bought a postal order worth seven shillings and sixpence. Mr Hem put it into an envelope and addressed it to Jack, his little nephew.

What a lot that smile had done already! It had made Mr Grim buy lots of new clothes and feel much happier. It had caused the tailor to feel most delighted, and had made him buy a postal order for seven shillings and sixpence.

Jack didn't expect such a wonderful birthday present from his uncle, the tailor. He didn't expect anything at all, because he knew that Uncle Hem was rather poor. As a matter of fact Jack had almost forgotten he was going to have a birthday, because he was so very unhappy about something.

That something was his puppy dog, Spot. You see, Spot was just over six months old, and so he should have had a licence. Every dog over that age has to have a licence bought for him at the post office. And poor Jack hadn't any money at all, and his father couldn't possibly pay for the licence! So he was dreadfully worried, because he loved Spot with all his heart

'Oh, Spot, if I can't buy you a licence someone will come and take you away from me!' he said, hugging the dog. 'All dogs must have licences, and you haven't got one. Oh, why did you grow big so quickly? I can't do without you!'

Spot licked his little master sorrowfully. He didn't know what was the matter, but it nearly broke his heart to see Jack cry.

And now you can imagine what Jack

felt like on the next day when his uncle's letter arrived with a postal order for seven shillings and sixpence! What a lot of money! Why – that was the price of a dog licence; it was, it was!

Inside the envelope with the money was a little note that said:

'Dear Jack,

I don't know what you want for your birthday, so here is some money. Spend it on anything you like, and be happy.

Your loving Uncle,
HEM.'

Jack flew round the kitchen in joy, waving the postal order about, and shouting excitedly to his father and to Spot, who was glad to see his little master so happy again. Out they went together to buy the licence, both of them running and jumping for all they were worth!

Jack bought the licence at the post office, and then went down by the river to go to his uncle's shop to thank him for his lovely present.

Now it so happened that Benny was running by the river too. He was going shopping for his mother again, just as

he had done the day before, and the path by the river was a short cut to the shops.

As he ran his foot caught against a piece of tree trunk, and over he went. He rolled down the river bank into the river! Splash! In he went, and the water closed right over his head. He came to the top and shouted for help.

Jack ran down to the water – but someone else was quicker! And that was Spot, the big puppy dog! He had seen Benny fall and had heard the splash. He loved his master so much that he wanted to help all other little boys, and he was

going to get Benny out of the river if he possibly could!

Splash! In he went too, and swam to Benny. He caught hold of the boy's coat in his strong teeth and swam steadily back to the bank with him, his four legs striking out gallantly. How everyone cheered! Lots of people had run down to the river when they had seen Benny fall in, and how glad they were when Spot got him safely to the bank. Jack dragged him up on the grass and Spot licked him all over.

'Good dog, Spot, good dog!' said Jack, very proud of his puppy. 'Oh, you deserve your seven-and-sixpenny licence – yes, you do!'

'He's the best dog in the world!' said Benny, hugging him. 'He saved me from being drowned! Look how wet I am!'

'Come with me to my uncle's,' said Jack. 'He lives nearby, and he'll dry you. He's awfully kind.'

So Benny went with Jack to his Uncle Hem's, and very soon he was standing in front of a big fire, wrapped in a shawl, whilst Mr Hem dried his clothes on a rack in the kitchen.

Whilst they were all talking nineteen to the dozen, who should come in but Mr Grim, to see how his new suits were getting on! He was *so* surprised to see Benny standing by the fire with a towel round his shoulders.

'Well, well,' he said, 'if it isn't the nice little boy who smiled at me yesterday! Well, well! What do you think your fine smile did for me, my boy? It made me feel so good that I came in here and ordered a whole lot of new clothes! Didn't I, Mr Hem?'

'You certainly did,' said the tailor. 'And your order made me very happy, because I knew then I could afford to send my little nephew here some money for his birthday. Did you get the postal order, Jack?'

'Oh, Uncle, yes, I did,' cried Jack, hugging the delighted tailor. 'I forgot to thank you for it because of all the excitement about Benny falling into the river.'

'What are you going to spend it on?' asked his uncle.

'I've spent it already!' said Jack. 'I've bought a dog licence for dear old Spot! We were just coming back from the post office when Benny fell into the river. And then Spot jumped in and saved him.'

Suddenly everyone was quiet. They were thinking. Most of all Benny was thinking. Presently he spoke.

'My own smile saved me!' he said. 'If I hadn't smiled at Mr Grim yesterday, he wouldn't have felt pleased and gone to buy his new clothes. If he hadn't gone to buy them, Mr Hem wouldn't have had the money to send to Jack. And if Jack hadn't had the money, he wouldn't have gone to buy a licence for Spot. And if he hadn't gone to buy the licence for Spot, he wouldn't have been by the river when I fell in and Spot wouldn't have been able to save me from drowning! It was all because of my smile – the smile my mother told me I ought to give to people, because I had nothing else to give but that!'

'What a wonderful thing!' said Mr Grim. 'Who would have thought a smile could do all that?'

'And I thought it was wasted!' said Benny. 'But it wasn't. Mother says smiles and kind words are never wasted, and she's right.'

Well, what do you think of that? But that wasn't all the smile did, by a long way! Because of that smile Jack, Benny and Spot became the greatest of friends. Mr Hem, the tailor, made such fine coats for Mr Grim that he became famous and had to take a larger shop – and as for Mr Grim himself, he was a different man! He became kind, generous and friendly, and all the children loved to meet him, for he never frowned as he used to do.

And all because of a smile!

Sly the cat and Smart the dog

THERE were once two animals who lived in the same house together. One was Sly the Cat, as cunning as her name – and the other was Smart the Dog, but he was *not* quite so clever as his name. Sly was always tricking him in some way, so she always got the best of everything.

One day they went out for a walk together. They were both very hungry, for they had had nothing to eat that morning. They sniffed the air and wondered what they might get to eat.

'What about going to the butcher's to see if there are any bones about?' asked Smart.

'No,' said Sly. 'You stole some sausages last time, so the butcher won't let us go anywhere near his shop.'

They trotted on together – and suddenly Sly lifted her nose in the air and sniffed hard.

'I smell something!' she said. 'Sniff, Smart, and see if you smell something, too.'

Smart sniffed. Yes, he smelt something. It was very strong.

'It's fish,' he said. 'Somewhere over by the stream, Sly. Let's go and look.'

Off they went, and soon came to where a dozen fish lay on the bank. Sly and Smart were delighted. Smart was going to gobble them up at once, but Sly spoke sharply.

'Be careful, Smart. They may be bad fish and might poison us. Don't eat in a hurry.'

Now Sly knew quite well that if the dog

began to eat the fish he would gobble them all up before she had even licked the tail of one! So she tried hard to think of a plan to stop him.

'So you really think they are bad fish?' asked Smart, sniffing. 'They do smell rather strong.'

'If we ate bad fish, we should have a pain and be dreadfully ill,' said Sly solemnly. 'What can we do?'

They sat and looked at one another. Sly felt sure the fish were quite all right, and she was anxious not to let the dog begin on them.

'I'll just take a little nibble at one end and see if it's all right,' said the dog, at last.

'No, don't! I couldn't bear to see you ill!' said the cat quickly. 'Let *me* have a nibble. I'll soon know if they are good or not!'

She ran to the fish and began to nibble at one. Then she sat back and pretended to taste what she had in her mouth. She suddenly made a face and began to rock to and fro and cry out:

'Oh, oh, fetch the doctor – the fish is bad! It's given me a dreadful pain! Oh,

I'm poisoned, I'm poisoned! Oh, fetch the doctor, quick!'

Smart was frightened. He ran to the cat to comfort her, but she waved him away and rocked herself to and fro again.

'Fetch the doctor, quick, fetch the doctor!' she wailed.

Smart ran off in a great hurry. The doctor lived quite three miles away, so he had a long way to go. He went as fast as he could, puffing and panting, his red tongue hanging out of the corner of his mouth.

'What a good thing we didn't gobble up *all* the fish!' he said to himself. 'My, we *should* have been ill!'

As soon as the dog was out of sight Sly began to laugh. She jumped up and went to the fish, and in a few moments she was having the best meal she had had for weeks. How she ate!

She ate a whole fish, and then she ate another. Then she started on a third – and she was just in the middle of it when a loud voice startled her, and she felt a heavy hand on her neck.

'How dare you steal my fish!' cried a cross voice. Sly twisted her head to see who had caught her, and saw that it was a fisherman! He had caught the fish that morning and had left them on the bank whilst he went to untangle his fishing-hook from a tree a little way off.

Poor Sly! The fisherman shook her this way and shook her that. He smacked her hard and he pulled her tail. She mewed loudly, but Smart the dog was too far away to hear her. No, it was a proper punishment for her!

The fisherman at last put her down on the ground again. Sly was so giddy that she sat where she was put, not daring to move. The fisherman gathered up the rest of the fish, put them into his basket, and went off.

Sly began to weep hot tears, for she felt so bad after her spanking. And what would Smart say when he came back and found all the fish gone?

Just as she was sitting there, feeling very sorry for herself, Smart came panting back with the doctor.

'Here's the patient!' he cried to the doctor. 'She nibbled a bit of bad fish, and

feels ill.' Then he looked for the rest of the fish to show the doctor. But it was gone!

'Where's the fish?' he barked angrily.

'A fisherman came and took it all,' said Sly. 'He said he had just caught it this morning.'

'Then it couldn't have been bad fish!' said Smart, in a rage. 'It was good fish and you played a trick on me! I don't believe that a fisherman came at all. I believe you ate all the fish yourself!'

With that he pounced on Sly and bit her tail so hard that she squeaked and fled. After her went Smart, yelping and barking for all he was worth. The doctor stood and stared after them, very angry to think he had come all that way for nothing.

'I shall send them in a great big bill for being so silly,' he said, as he tramped home again.

As for Smart and Sly, they soon made up their quarrel and were friends again – but you may be sure that Smart made *Sly* pay the doctor's bill!

The two cocks

ONCE upon a time there were two cocks in a farmyard. They were fine fellows, called Doodle and Doo. Their red combs stood up from their heads, and their tail-feathers sprouted grandly, shining now blue and now green.

Their voices were very loud. They cried: 'Cock-a-doodle-do!' at the very first peep of dawn, and woke up all the farm folk at once. They strutted over the yard, their heads held up and their combs glowing red. Sometimes they fought one another and then the feathers flew in all directions.

They lived with twenty-two red hens. The hens had no fine tail-feathers, but they were pretty, for all that. How they scratched and scraped in the earth, looking for a tiny grain to gobble up! How they ran when they heard Mistress Susan rattling the pail in which she brought their food twice a day!

The two cocks were so alike that you really couldn't tell one from the other – except in their manners. Ah, you could tell which was Doodle and which was Doo then! They might look the same from beak to tail, but their manners were quite different.

Doodle was a greedy cock who didn't care two grains of corn for any of his hens. He scraped in the earth just as they did and if he found a nice big piece of corn, what did he do? Did he call his hens to share it? No, not he! He gave a greedy squawk and gobbled it up himself.

And when Mistress Susan flung handfuls of corn to the fowls, did Doodle see that all the hens got their full share before he ate any? No – the greedy, ill-mannered bird pushed aside the hungry hens and gobbled up all he could, even going so far as to snatch a specially big grain of corn out of a hen's beak! He was not a nice bird at all.

But Doo was quite different. If he scraped up a grain of maize he called to his hens at once and they all came running. Then he would drop the maize in front of a hen and she would gobble it up gratefully. When Mistress Susan threw the food into the yard Doo never picked up the tiniest piece himself until he was quite sure every single one of his hens had had enough. Then he would hurriedly have his meal.

Now one day the farmer said that he wanted a bird for his dinner.

'Master's coming to sup with us tonight,' he told his wife. 'So we'll have one of those two cocks for dinner, Mistress.'

'Very well, George,' said Mistress Susan. 'Which one will you have?'

'It doesn't matter,' said the farmer. 'They are as like as two peas.'

'Oh, no, Father, they're not!' cried his little girl. 'Doodle is a horrid bird. He is greedy and spiteful, and has no manners at all. But Doo is gentle and kind. He always lets the hens eat first.'

'Then we'll have Doodle for supper,' said the farmer. 'Do you know which is which, wife?'

'No, I don't,' said Mistress Susan. 'But

I'll take our Annie with me and she'll tell me.'

So Annie went with her mother to the yard. The two cocks were standing in the sun, enjoying the warmth. They looked exactly alike.

'Well, well,' said Mistress Susan. 'There's no telling which is which, Annie dear.'

'Watch,' said Annie, and she threw a handful of corn into the yard. Oh, what a scramble there was! How the hens squawked and clucked! And dear me, what a disgrace the cock Doodle was! He gobbled up all the grains he could see and pecked at the hen next to him, pulling away a tuft of feathers from her neck.

But Doo helped the hens to find the grain. He gave two pieces to the smallest hen of all, who wasn't very good at pushing and pecking. He really was a perfect gentleman.

'There, Mother!' said Annie, pointing. 'See what a difference there is in the cocks! Don't eat Doo, he's so good and kind. Eat Doodle, the greedy ill-natured bird!'

So Doodle was made into a pie for supper, and Doo was left with the hens. Nobody missed Doodle or wanted him back. As for Doo he is still alive, and looking after his hens as well as ever.

And now mother hens say to greedy, ill-mannered chicks: 'Be careful! Bad manners are made into a pie, but good ones live for ever!'

Mr Miggle's spectacles

ONCE upon a time there was a gnome called Mr Miggle. He thought a lot of himself, and he hoped other people did too – but they didn't! They thought Mr Miggle was a fat, greedy, mean old gnome, who always pretended he was too poor to help anyone.

Mr Miggle was vain. He felt sure everyone liked him and admired him, but he did wish they would say so. Nobody ever told him he was good-looking, and nobody said he was kind or good.

'I suppose they are too shy to say so to me,' he thought, as he walked proudly down the village street, dressed in a new yellow suit, tied up with red ribbons all down the front. 'How I wish I knew what everyone was thinking about me! It would be lovely to know. I expect they are thinking how fine I look, and what a grand gnome I am!'

Now it so happened that on that day a pedlar came to Mr Miggle's village, selling all kinds of strange things. He called at Mr Miggle's house after tea, and Mr Miggle looked at his things.

'Here's a broom that will sweep by itself,' said the pedlar, showing Miggle a little yellow broom. 'Or here's a jug which is always full of new milk.'

'No, thanks,' said Mr Miggle. 'I don't want those.'

'Well, what about a pair of spectacles that will tell you what everyone is thinking about you?' said the pedlar, picking

up a little red case and opening it. In it lay a pair of big round spectacles with very peculiar glass that twinkled and blinked all the time.

'Oooh!' said Mr Miggle. 'Just what I want! How much?'

'Three pieces of gold!' said the pedlar. 'They are very rare, you know.'

Mr Miggle put the spectacles on and looked hard at the pedlar. The man immediately thought something nice about

Miggle, for he knew the gnome was reading his thoughts.

Mr Miggle saw what he thought – the pedlar was thinking: 'What a nice gnome! I'm sure he will be sensible enough to buy my wonderful spectacles, for they are very cheap indeed!'

Mr Miggle wasn't clever enough to know that the pedlar was thinking these things on purpose, and he was very pleased. He paid the gold without a word and the pedlar went off, chuckling to himself, thinking of the dreadful shocks that Miggle would have when he put the spectacles on and found out what people REALLY thought of him!

Miggle was most excited. He could hardly sleep that night for thinking of the lovely time he would have the next day, finding out what everyone thought of him.

'I shall put on my new suit again,' he said to himself. 'I look nice in that. Then I will walk down the street with my spectacles on and see what everyone is thinking about me.'

So the next morning he put on his fine yellow suit, popped his pointed hat on, and settled his new spectacles on his nose. Then out he went down the street.

The first person he met was old Dame Wimple. Miggle smiled at her and she nodded back. She didn't say a word. Miggle looked at her through his glasses to see what she was thinking – and my, what a shock he got!

'Silly, fat old gnome!' the old dame was thinking. 'I suppose he thinks he looks fine in that awful suit. What a sight he looks!'

Miggle nearly cried out in horror. Could old Dame Wimple really be thinking that? No, no, the glasses must be making some mistake!

Round the corner he met Skip and Jump, the little boy pixies who lived at Hallo Cottage. He smiled at them, and they said good morning to him most politely. Mr Miggle looked through his glasses to see what they were really thinking, and again he got a most terrible shock.

'Nasty, mean old thing!' Skip was thinking. 'He never gives a little pixie even a ha'penny!'

'What an ugly face old Miggle's got!' Jump was thinking. 'I should hate to meet him at night in a dark corner!'

Well! Miggle was so surprised that he stood quite still and stared at the two little pixies. They were frightened and ran away. Miggle heaved a great sigh and went on.

'I suppose children always think silly things like that,' he said to himself. 'It's

no use taking any notice of them. It's the grown-ups that matter.'

At the roadside stood a brownie, selling red apples. Mr Miggle looked at him through his glasses, hoping to see some really nice thoughts in his head. But, no, again he was disappointed.

'It's no use asking this mean-looking old gnome to buy my nice apples,' the brownie was thinking. 'He looks a real miser, although he is so fat.'

Mr Miggle was shocked. Did he really look like a miser? He looked into a mirror set in a shop window. Yes, his

mouth did look rather thin and mean. Oh, dear, he wasn't having a very nice morning!

Ah, here came Mr Snoop, his friend. *Now* he would read some nice thoughts, surely. He shook hands with Snoop and looked at him through his glasses. Oh goodness! Mr Snoop was thinking no better thoughts than the others.

'So he's got a new suit again,' Snoop was thinking. 'Why does he always have his suits so tight they look as if they were bursting? And why does Miggle eat so much? He really is much too fat. I'm sure

I don't know why I'm friends with him. He's a mean, greedy fellow and I don't really like him at all.'

Snoop was very much surprised to see Miggle burst into tears and hurry down the street without a word. He had no idea that the fat little gnome could see what he was thinking and had been very much upset by it.

'Well, well,' thought Snoop, 'what next? He really is a silly chap, that Miggle.'

Miggle dried his eyes under his glasses and walked up the hill towards Mrs Lemon's cottage. Mrs Lemon was out in her garden watering her flowers. Miggle hardly dared to look at her in case he read something horrid about himself.

'But she's the kindest person in the village,' he thought. 'So she's sure to be thinking something nice about me. I'll see if she is.'

He said good morning to Mrs Lemon and read her thoughts. Poor Miggle! He had no luck that morning for Mrs Lemon, kindhearted as she was, was not thinking very nice things about the foolish, fat gnome.

'Here comes old greedy Miggle,' she was thinking. 'Poor old fellow! I wonder if he guesses how everyone laughs at him and dislikes him. I believe he thinks we all like him. If only he knew what we think, he would get a dreadful shock!'

Miggle *did* get a dreadful shock! He looked at Mrs Lemon as if he couldn't believe his ears and eyes. She was astonished.

'What's the matter?' she asked. 'Are you ill? Come into my garden and sit down for a bit.'

Mr Miggle read what she was thinking.

'Miggle looks ill,' she was thinking. 'I suppose as usual he's been eating too much. What a dreadful fellow he is, to be sure!'

Miggle stopped at the gate and spoke sadly to Mrs Lemon.

'I can see what you are thinking, Lucy Lemon,' he said. 'I have magic spectacles

on. You have been thinking I am a greedy fellow, whom nobody likes. Ah, well, perhaps you are right.'

Mrs Lemon was astonished. She looked at Miggle's spectacles and saw that they were magic ones. She was sorry for the unhappy gnome, for she knew what a lot of shocks he must have had that morning.

'Come in for a minute,' she said kindly. 'I didn't mean you to see my thoughts – but people can't very well help their thoughts, can they?'

Miggle came in and sat down on a bench. He took off his glasses and looked at Mrs Lemon.

'Am I a very horrid fellow? he asked.

'You are rather,' said Mrs Lemon, 'but you needn't be. If only you wouldn't think so much of yourself, Miggle, and would think a little more of other people, you'd be all right. And you shouldn't eat so much, you know – you're getting fat and ugly. You used to be such a good-looking gnome!'

Miggle was very sad.

'Do you think I could ever be nice?' he asked.

'It's never too late to mend,' said Mrs Lemon. 'You mustn't blame other people for what they think of you, you know. It is you that have made their thoughts about you. The people in this village are kindly folk, and it's your own fault if they think unkindly about you. What about trying to turn over a new leaf, Miggle? Try for a month and then put on the magic glasses again!'

Miggle said he would try. He put his glasses into their case, thanked Mrs Lemon for helping him and went sadly home. He sat down by his fire and made all sorts of plans.

He wouldn't be so greedy. He would take good long walks each day to make himself thinner. He would be kind and generous to the children and to the poor people. He would ask Snoop, his friend, to help him.

Poor Mr Miggle! He tried hard for a month and it wasn't easy. Snoop and Mrs Miggle helped him, and at last he really felt a bit different. He looked for his magic glasses to put on to see if people were thinking kinder thoughts about him – and they weren't there!

He had lost them – so he never knew what other people were thinking about him after all – but as he really is different, I expect their thoughts are different, too. Don't you?

Nobody knows where those glasses went to. If you should ever come across them, what sort of thoughts would you read in other people's minds if you put those spectacles on? I wonder!